Welcome mia!

MADELINE

Every little girl needs
to know madeline ...
and someday go to Paris!

love - Mary & Renn

MADELINE

story & pictures by
Ludwig Bemelmans

PUFFIN BOOKS

OTHER *MADELINE* BOOKS YOU MIGHT ENJOY

———————

PUFFIN BOOKS

Published by the Penguin Group

Penguin Putnam Inc., 375 Hudson Street, New York, New York 10014, U.S.A.

Penguin Books Ltd, 27 Wrights Lane, London W8 5TZ, England

Penguin Books Australia Ltd, Ringwood, Victoria, Australia

Penguin Books Canada Ltd, 10 Alcorn Avenue, Toronto, Ontario, Canada M4V 3B2

Penguin Books (N.Z.) Ltd, 182-190 Wairau Road, Auckland 10, New Zealand

Penguin Books Ltd, Registered Offices: Harmondsworth, Middlesex, England

First published by Simon and Schuster, 1939

First published by The Viking Press, 1958

Published in a Viking Seafarer Edition, 1969

Reprinted 1971, 1972, 1973, 1974, 1975

Published in Picture Puffins, 1977

This edition published in Puffin Books, 1998

13 15 17 19 20 18 16 14 12

THE LIBRARY OF CONGRESS HAS CATALOGED THE PREVIOUS PUFFIN EDITION AS FOLLOWS:

Bemelmans, Ludwig. Madeline

Summary: Madeline, smallest and naughtiest of the twelve little charges of
Miss Clavel, wakes up one night with an attack of appendicitis.

[1. France—Fiction. 2. Sick—Fiction. 3. Stories in rhyme] 1. Title

[PZ8.3.B425Mag8] [E] 76-50664

ISBN 0 14 050.198 3

This edition ISBN 0-14-056439-X

Printed in the United States of America

MADELINE

In an old house in Paris

that was covered with vines

lived twelve little girls in two straight lines.

In two straight lines they broke their bread

and brushed their teeth

and went to bed.

They smiled at the good

and frowned at the bad

and sometimes they were very sad.

They left the house

at half past nine

in two straight lines

in rain

or shine—

the smallest one was Madeline.

She was not afraid of mice—

she loved winter, snow, and ice.

To the tiger in the zoo
Madeline just said, "Pooh-pooh,"

and nobody knew so well
how to frighten Miss Clavel.

In the middle of one night
Miss Clavel turned on her light
and said, "Something is not right!"

Little Madeline sat in bed,
cried and cried; her eyes were red.

And soon after Dr. Cohn
came, he rushed out to the phone

and he dialed: DANton-ten-six—

"Nurse," he said, "it's an appendix!"

Everybody had to cry—
not a single eye was dry.

Madeline was in his arm
in a blanket safe and warm.

In a car with a red light

they drove out into the night.

Madeline woke up two hours
later, in a room with flowers.

Madeline soon ate and drank.

On her bed there was a crank,

and a crack on the ceiling had the habit
of sometimes looking like a rabbit.

Outside were birds, trees, and sky—
and so ten days passed quickly by.

One nice morning Miss Clavel said—

"Isn't this a fine—

day to visit

Madeline."

VISITORS FROM TWO TO FOUR
read a sign outside her door.

Tiptoeing with solemn face,

with some flowers and a vase,

in they walked and then said, "Ahhh,"

when they saw the toys and candy

and the dollhouse from Papa.

But the biggest surprise by far—
on her stomach
was a scar!

"Good-by," they said, "we'll come again."

and the little girls left in the rain.

They went home and broke their bread

brushed their teeth

and went to bed.

In the middle of the night
Miss Clavel turned on the light
and said, "Something is not right!"

And afraid of a disaster

Miss Clavel ran fast

and faster,

and she said, "Please children do—
tell me what is troubling you?"

And all the little girls cried, "Boohoo,
we want to have our appendix out, too!"

"Good night, little girls!
Thank the lord you are well!
And now go to sleep!"
said Miss Clavel.

And she turned out the light—

and closed the door—

and that's all there is—

there isn't any more.

HERE is a list for those who may wish to identify the Paris scenes Ludwig Bemelmans has pictured in this book.

On the cover and in one of the
illustrations
THE EIFFEL TOWER

In the picture of the lady feeding
the horse
THE OPERA

A gendarme chases a jewel thief across
THE PLACE VENDOME

A wounded soldier at
THE HOTEL DES INVALIDES

A rainy day in front of
NOTRE DAME

A sunny day looking across
THE GARDENS AT THE LUXEMBOURG

Behind the little girls skating is
THE CHURCH OF THE SACRE COEUR

A man is feeding birds in
THE TUILERIES GARDENS FACING
THE LOUVRE